Frédéric
Brrémaud

Federico
Bertolucci

Little TAILS

In the Forest

with
Chipper & Squizzo

WRITTEN BY
FRÉDÉRIC BRRÉMAUD

ILLUSTRATED BY
FEDERICO BERTOLUCCI

TRANSLATION ADAPTED BY
MIKE KENNEDY

MAGNETIC PRESS

MIKE KENNEDY, *President/Publisher*

WES HARRIS, *Vice President*

DAVID DISSANAYAKE, *PR & Marketing*

4910 N. WINTHROP AVE #3S

CHICAGO, IL 60640

WWW.MAGNETIC-PRESS.COM

LITTLE TAILS IN THE FOREST (VOLUME 1)

SEPTEMBER 2016. FIRST PRINTING

ISBN: 978-1-942367-25-3

FIRST PUBLISHED IN FRANCE BY EDITIONS CLAIR DE LUNE

ALL CONTENT © 2014 FRÉDÉRIC BRRÉMAUD AND FEDERICO BERTOLUCCI

WHAT? NO! THOSE ARE WILD BOAR TRACKS!

WHAT'S A BOAR?

I'M A BOAR! WE DIG THROUGH THE DIRT TO FIND ACORNS AND WORMS... YOU WANNA TRY?

COME ON! IT'S FUN! AND WE GET MUDDY, TOO!

HAHAH, THANKS! MAYBE LATER...

WHEW — OKAY, NOW THAT IT'S STARTING TO GET DARK, WE HAVE TO BE CAREFUL OUT HERE IN THE WOODS . . .

BUT WE SHOULDN'T BE AFRAID. ANIMALS AREN'T BAD, THEY'RE JUST —

AAAAHHH! ARE YOU CRAZY?

WHAT? YOU SAID ANIMALS AREN'T BAD . . .

JUST RUN! I'LL EXPLAIN LATER!

LISTEN, WHEN YOU DON'T KNOW AN ANIMAL, YOU NEED TO BE CAREFUL . . .

BUT THAT SNAKE LOOKED NICE . . . SHE HAD A SORT OF SMILE . . .

MAYBE SHE WAS NICE, BUT LIKE ALL WILD ANIMALS, SHE NEEDS TO SURVIVE . . .

. . . AND THAT MEANS FINDING SOMETHING TO EAT!

GAH! OKAY, I SEE YOUR POINT.

LET'S NOT WORRY ABOUT IT ANY MORE. AFTER THE OWL, THE SNAKE, AND THE FOX, I DON'T THINK THERE'S ANYTHING LEFT TO BE AFRAID OF . . .

EXCEPT MAYBE . . . UM . . .

WHAT?

HOOOOWL!

WOLVES!

!

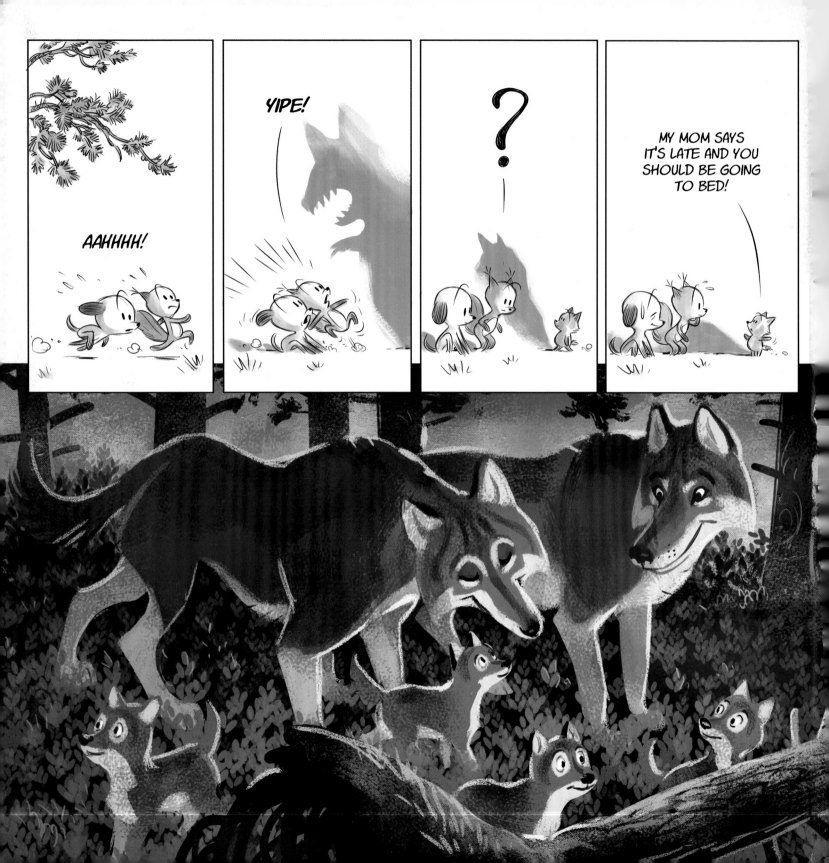

BEAR

IN COLD REGIONS, AT THE FIRST SNOWFALL, THE BEAR WILL TAKE REFUGE IN HIS LAIR TO HIBERNATE. HIS HEART RATE SLOWS, AND HE DOESN'T EAT, OR EVEN GO TO THE BATHROOM, FOR SEVERAL MONTHS. BUT HE ISN'T JUST SLEEPING -- UNLIKE SOME OTHER ANIMALS THAT HIBERNATE, HIS SENSES ARE STILL AWAKE, AND IF THE SUN COMES OUT, HE MIGHT EVEN GO OUTSIDE FOR A BIT!

SEVERAL MONTHS WITHOUT EATING?! WOW!

DEER

EVERY YEAR, IN EARLY SPRING, THE DEER SHEDS ITS ANTLERS. FORTUNATELY, THEY GROW BACK BETWEEN MARCH AND JULY. THEIR SIZE DOESN'T REFLECT THE AGE OF THE ANIMAL, BUT IS MORE A SIGN OF STRENGTH -- A YOUNG AND HEALTHY DEER WILL OFTEN HAVE THE MOST IMPRESSIVE ANTLERS.

HEDGEHOG

THE SPINES ON A HEDGEHOG AREN'T REALLY SHARP LIKE A PORCUPINE. THEY ARE REALLY VERY THICK HAIRS THAT HE CAN BRISTLE WHEN HE FEELS THREATENED, SO HE LOOKS SHARP AND DANGEROUS. BUT WHEN HE IS CALM AND QUIET, HE LOWERS THE SPINES AND BECOMES VERY SOFT...

OWL

THE OWL HAS BIG EYES ON THE SIDE OF HER HEAD THAT SHE CAN'T MOVE. BUT HER NECK IS SO ELASTIC THAT IT CAN TURN ALMOST ALL THE WAY AROUND, SO SHE CAN LOOK BEHIND HER AND ALMOST STRAIGHT UP, WHICH IS VERY USEFUL TO SEE WHAT'S ON THE TOP BRANCH ABOVE HER...

FOX

THE FOX IS AN OMNIVORE. THAT MEANS, LIKE US, HE CAN EAT ALMOST ANYTHING. RABBITS, BIRDS, EARTHWORMS, BUGS, GRASSHOPPERS, FRUIT... YOU NAME IT! WHEN A FOX IS FEEDING HER YOUNG, SHE CAN HUNT UP TO 10,000 RODENTS IN A SINGLE SEASON. 10,000!

SKUNK

THE SKUNK POSSESSES A TERRIBLE WEAPON: TWO SMALL GLANDS LOCATED UNDER THE TAIL WHICH SECRETES A SUBSTANCE THAT SMELLS REALLY BAD AND IRRITATES THE EYES. WHEN SHE FEELS THREATENED, SHE LIFTS HER TAIL TO LOOK BIGGER. AND IF THAT ISN'T ENOUGH TO SCARE AWAY A THREAT, IT SQUIRTS THE NAUSEATING LIQUID AT THE ENEMY. MOST PREDATORS FEAR SKUNKS BECAUSE IF THEY GET SQUIRTED, THEY NOT ONLY FEEL SICK, BUT THEIR PREY CAN SPOT THEM FROM VERY FAR AWAY. THEY COULD GO HUNGRY FOR DAYS!

SQUIRREL

THE SQUIRREL'S TAIL IS VERY USEFUL. IT HELPS THEM BALANCE WHEN THEY JUMP, AND IF THEY FALL, IT CAN ACT A LITTLE LIKE A PARACHUTE. IT IS ALSO A GREAT UMBRELLA TO PROTECT THEM FROM THE RAIN OR BRIGHT SUN, AND IT MAKES A GREAT SCARF WHEN IT'S COLD. IT IS ALSO A COZY PILLOW WHEN THEY CURL UP INSIDE A TREE TRUNK. IT REALLY IS A MULTIPURPOSE TOOL!

WOLF

WOLVES ARE SOCIAL ANIMALS. THEY LIVE IN A PACK AND OBEY A HIERARCHY WITH VERY PRECISE RULES. WHEN THE PACK IS MOVING, WOLVES FOLLOW THEIR LEADER SO CLOSELY THAT SOMETIMES, AFTER A PACK OF WOLVES HAS PASSED, IF YOU LOOK AT THEIR FOOTPRINTS, YOU MIGHT THINK THERE WAS ONLY ONE WOLF!

I HIT TREE TRUNKS WITH MY BEAK TO FIND BUGS AND TO MARK MY TERRITORY. WHO AM I?

UM . . . A SPARROW?

NOPE! I'M A **WOOD-PECKER**!

BUT YOU WERE PRETTY CLOSE, SO I'LL GIVE YOU POINTS ANYWAY . . .